#8 "Tinker Bell and her Stories for a Rainy Day"

Contents

PAPERCUTZ™

NEW YORK

"Impossible Portraits"
Script: Augusto Macchetto
Revised Dialogue: Cortney Faye Powell
Pencils: Augusto Macchetto
Inks: Cristina Giorgilli
Color: Stefania Santi
Letters: Janice Chiang
Page 5 Art:
Pencils: Gianluca Barone
Inks: Marina Baggio
Color: Andrea Cagol

"Dulcie's Secret Ingredients""
Script: Paola Mulazzi
Revised Dialogue: Cortney Faye Powell
Pencils: Elisabetta Melaranci
Inks: Marina Baggio
Color: Stefania Santi
Letters: Janice Chiang
Page 18 Art:
Pencils: Caterina Giorgetti
Inks: Roberta Zanotta
Color: Andrea Cagol

"Butterfly Wings"
Script: Silvia Gianatti
Revised Dialogue: Cortney Faye Powell
Pencils: Emilio Urbano and Manuela Razzi
Inks: Roberta Zanotta
Color: Stefania Santi
Letters: Janice Chiang
Page 31 Art:
Pencils: Gianluca Barone
Inks: Marina Baggio
Color: Andrea Cagol

"Tinker Bell and her Stories For a Rainy Day"
Script: Augusto Macchetto
Revised Dialogue: Cortney Faye Powell
Pencils: Elisabetta Melaranci
Inks: Cristina Giorgilli
Color: Stefania Santi
Letters: Janice Chiang
Page 44 Art:
Pencils: Caterina Giorgetti
Inks: Marina Baggio
Color: Andrea Cagol

Preview of "A Fairy Might Be Near"
Script: Augusto Maccetto
Revised Dialogue: Cortney Faye Powell
Pencils and Inks: Antonello Dalena
Color: Kawaii Creative Studio
Lettering: Janice Chiang

Nelson Design Group – Production
Special Thanks – Jesse Post and Shiho Tilley
Michael Petranek – Associate Editor
Jim Salicrup
Editor-in-Chief

ISBN: 978-1-59707-303-5 paperback edition
ISBN: 978-1-59707-304-2 hardcover edition

Printed in Singapore. October 2012
by Tien Wah Press PTE LTD
4 Pandan Crescent
Singapore 128475

Distributed by Macmillan

First Papercutz Printing

IMPOSSIBLE PORTRAITS

QUEEN CLARION IS LOOKING FOR A SPECIAL ROOM IN THE HOME TREE...

IT'S DECORATED WITH THE FINEST MOTHER-OF-PEARL!

YES... THIS ROOM MIGHT DO...

POLISHED BY OUR MOST SKILLFUL FAIRIES!

YES, YES, IT IS ALL OF THAT! BUT IT'S ALSO A BIT EMPTY... ONE COULD FEEL QUITE LONELY IN HERE!

THE QUEEN'S LOOKING FOR A ROOM TO TURN INTO HER STUDY!

OH!

- 10 -

- 12 -

ALL THE FAIRIES SEEM TO HAVE A WORLD OF THINGS TO DO! THEY CAN'T EVEN STAND STILL FOR A MOMENT. HOW AM I SUPPOSED TO PAINT THEM?!

GO AHEAD! PAINT ME!

ALL RIGHT! THE LIGHT IS VERY NICE, TOO...

OH, NO! THE WARM GLOW OF SUNSET! IT'LL BE NIGHT SOON! AND PORTRAITS CAN'T BE PAINTED IN THE DARK!

WELL, I DON'T HAVE ANYTHING TO DO RIGHT NOW!

POOR BESS! WELL, I'LL FLY TO SEE YOU FIRST THING TOMORROW MORNING SO YOU CAN PAINT ME!

YOU MEAN IT? THANKS, PRILLA!

WAIT, I PROMISED I'D HELP LILY PICK BLACKBERRIES AT DAWN!

LATER...

HI, BESS! WHY ARE YOUR WINGS SO DROOPY?

DON'T WORRY. I'M NOT SURPRISED...

I'VE WASTED A LOT OF TIME, FIRA! AND I HAVEN'T PAINTED ANYTHING!

WELL, MAKE YOURSELF USEFUL, THEN! HELP ME ARRANGE THE FIREFLIES FOR THE NIGHT!

UM... FIREFLIES...

OF COURSE! YOU'VE GIVEN ME A *BRILLIANT* IDEA!

CLEARLY I HAVE! I'M A LIGHT-TALENT FAIRY...

WORKING HARD, BESS? OR HARDLY WORKING?

I'M READY FOR BESS TO PAINT MY PORTRAIT, BUT I CAN'T FIND HER ANYWHERE!

SAME HERE. LET'S LOOK TOGETHER.

UM... THERE SHE IS...

COME ON, SLEEPYHEAD, YOU MUST BE TIRED...

LOOK AT HER! SHE SURE IS WORKING HARD, HUH?

YOU SNOOZE, YOU LOSE...

BESS! MY OWL FRIEND SLEEPS HERE... COULDN'T YOU NAP SOMEWHERE ELSE?

OH... I'D FLY BACKWARDS! I'LL MOVE!

HOO! HOO!

BUT...

BESS! I JUST PLANTED SOMETHING THERE!

I'D FLY BACKWARDS, LILY!

SOON THE QUEEN DISCOVERS THAT BESS IS SLEEPING ALL THE TIME!

I THOUGHT YOU HAD PAINTING TALENT... NOT SNORING TALENT!

~YAWN~! THE THING IS, I WAS DOING THE PAINTINGS AT NIGHT, QUEEN CLARION!

THE FAIRIES HAVE TOO MUCH TO DO DURING THE DAYTIME, I DECIDED TO PAINT THEIR PORTRAITS WHILE THEY WERE SLEEPING!

"OUR FIREFLY FRIENDS HELPED ME...

- 29 -

- 36 -

- 38 -

THE END

TINKER BELL AND HER STORIES FOR A RAINY DAY

IF YOU TOSS SOMETHING INTO THE POND, THE RIPPLE MAKES A *CIRCLE*...

BUT WATER-TALENT FAIRIES CAN MAKE *ALL KINDS* OF SHAPES!

OH, RANI, WHAT A MAGICAL PRESENT! WHERE DID YOU GET YOUR INSPIRATION?

"AND SO, MY PRESENT IS GOING TO BE... TELLING THE QUEEN HOW MUCH I LOVE HER WITH RIPPLES!"

OH, HEE, HEE, IT JUST CAME TO ME WITH A PLOP!

NOW, YOU TELL A STORY, TINK!

ALL RIGHT! I'LL TELL YOU ABOUT WHEN I FIRST ARRIVED IN PIXIE HOLLOW!

LIKE ALL FAIRIES, I WAS BORN FROM A CHILD'S FIRST LAUGH!

"I REMEMBER THAT IT WAS A WONDERFUL EVENING ON THE MAINLAND!"

"THE STARS WERE TWINKLING SO BRIGHT... ESPECIALLY THE SECOND STAR TO THE RIGHT!"

WATCH OUT FOR

PAPERCUT乙™

Welcome to the eighth (collect 'em all!) enchanting DISNEY FAIRIES graphic novel from Papercutz, the folks dedicated to creating great graphic novels for all ages. I'm Jim Salicrup, your pixilated Editor-in-Chief, and one-time guest on the Mickey Mouse Club!

While we're relatively certain most of you are well aware of exactly who Tinker Bell and her fellow fairies are, we're not too sure you're fully aware of who and what Papercutz is. Well, fear not, I'm more than happy to shed a little light on that mystery. It all started in 2005, when Papercutz publisher Terry Nantier and I got together to start a new comics publishing company that would produce material for all ages. After all, both Terry and I have loved comics since we were kids, and it seemed that there was too few comics being published back then that were suitable for all ages. The reason for that is really strange. In a nutshell, comics were being created and produced by adults and sold and distributed to comicbook stores run by adults and sold to their primarily adult customers. While that's all well and good if you're an adult, we wondered about where the next generation of comics fans would come if nothing was being produced for younger fans?

Furthermore, there was very little being produced for female comics fans. Again, the reason was strange—very few females would shop in comicbook stores, so very few comics were produced for female audiences. It was a crazy situation! But everything changed when regular bookstores started giving shelf space to graphic novels and Manga. Finally the comics and their intended audience (that's you!) we're starting to come together. So, while overall that's a wonderful thing, it too has its limitations. For example, if one of our graphic novels is located in the "childrens section" some older folks may assume the graphic novel is too juvenile for them. As you can see, there is no simple solution yet, but at least we're making progress. More and more comicbook stores are realizing what a wonderful idea it is to carry such graphic novels as DISNEY FAIRIES, GERONIMO STILTON, and THE SMURFS (Not to mention DANCE CLASS, ERNEST & REBECCA, GARFIELD & Co, and NINJAGO) and we're very thankful for that!

There is a little something you can do to help. It's not that difficult. All you need to do, if you're interested in any of those Papercutz graphic novels just mentioned, is to ask your friendly comicbook store worker or bookstore employee to order the books you're interested in. Chances are they'll be happy to do that for you, and it'll help convince them that there are lots of people out there who are looking for this type of material. Of course, if you're favorite comicbook shop or bookstore already carries plenty of Papercutz graphic novels, then it certainly won't hurt to let them know how thankful you are that they do.

It's been several years since Papercutz started, and the good news is that there seems to be more and more comics and graphic novels being created for all ages. Partly that's thanks to you—for supporting titles such as DISNEY FAIRIES. And on behalf of everyone at Papercutz, we're very thankful to you for your continued support!

So, until we meet again in DISNEY FAIRIES #9 " Tinker Bell and Her Magical Arrival," don't forget to keep believing in "faith, trust, and pixie dust"!

Thanks,

Jim

Don't miss DISNEY FAIRIES Graphic Novel #9 "Tinker Bell and her Magical Arrival"